Katie Woo

Boo, Katie Woo!

by Fran Manushkin

illustrated by Tammie Lyon

PICTURE WINDOW BOOKS

a capstone imprint

Katie Woo is published by Picture Window Books,
151 Good Counsel Drive, P.O. Box 669
Mankato, Minnesota, MN 56002
www.capstonepub.com

Library of Congress Cataloging-in-Publication Data is
available on the Library of Congress website.
ISBN: 978-1-4048-5987-6 (library binding)
ISBN: 978-1-4048-6366-8 (paperback)

Summary: Katie is disappointed when she
doesn't scare anyone on Halloween.

Art Director: Kay Fraser
Graphic Designer: Emily Harris

Photo Credits
Fran Manushkin, pg. 26
Tammie Lyon, pg. 26

Table of Contents

Chapter 1
Halloween Plans

Halloween was coming.

Katie asked Pedro and

JoJo, "What are you going

to be?"

"I'm going to be a cowgirl," said JoJo.

"I'm going to be a magician," said Pedro.

"What are you going to be, Katie?"

"A monster!" shouted

Katie. "I'll scare everyone

silly!"

Chapter 2

The Big Night

Finally, it was Halloween!

Katie, Pedro, and JoJo

went trick-or-treating

together.

Katie rang the first bell.

A girl answered.

"Boo!" shouted Katie
Woo.

The girl laughed. "You
don't scare me!" she said.

"I can do a trick!" said
JoJo.

She twirled her cowgirl
rope and jumped in and out
of it.

"Cool!" said the girl. She gave JoJo lots of candy.

Katie, Pedro, and JoJo

went to the next house. A

boy answered this time.

"Boo!" shouted Katie

Woo.

"You don't scare me!" said

the boy.

"I can do a magic trick," said Pedro.

He made a spoon bend by just looking at it!

"Cool trick!" The boy smiled. He gave Pedro a lot of candy.

As they
walked to the
next house,
their friend

Jake came running by.

"Have you seen a little
brown kitten?" he asked.
"She ran away, and I can't
find her."

"We haven't," said Katie.
"I'm sorry."

Just then, the three friends

heard a spooky shriek!

"Yikes!" yelled JoJo.

"Don't be scared," said Katie. "It's only a squeaky gate swinging in the wind."

Chapter 3

Spooks and Screams

As they walked along,

Katie said, "I'm not having

any fun. I haven't scared

anyone."

At the next house, Katie yelled "BOO!" as loud as she could.

"Hi, Katie!" said Barry, a boy in her class. "I knew it was you!"

Katie was so mad, she

stomped her feet.

"Look!" said Pedro. "The

moon is out. It looks nice and

spooky."

"It's too spooky!" said JoJo
with a shiver.

"Yikes!" yelled Katie.
"Something's wiggling on
the ground."

"It's a snake!" she screamed.

Katie climbed up a tree to get away.

"That's not a snake," said

JoJo. "It's the shadow of my

jump rope."

"Meow!" came a sound

close to Katie in the tree.

"It's Jake's lost kitten,"

Katie said. "It's a good thing

I climbed this tree!"

"Don't be scared," Katie

told the kitten. "I'm going to

take you home."

Jake hugged his kitten over and over. "How did you find her?" he asked.

Katie smiled. "Let's just say it was a trick that turned into a treat."

It was a very happy Halloween!

About the Author

Fran Manushkin is the author of many popular picture books, including *How Mama Brought the Spring; Baby, Come Out!; Latkes and Applesauce: A Hanukkah Story;* and *The Tushy Book.* There is a real Katie Woo — she's Fran's great-niece — but she never gets in half the trouble of the Katie Woo in the books. Fran writes on her beloved Mac computer in New York City, without the help of her two naughty cats, Cookie and Goldy.

About the Illustrator

Tammie Lyon began her love for drawing at a young age while sitting at the kitchen table with her dad. She continued her love of art and eventually attended the Columbus College of Art and Design, where she earned a bachelors degree in fine art. After a brief career as a professional ballet dancer, she decided to devote herself full time to illustration. Today she lives with her husband, Lee, in Cincinnati, Ohio. Her dogs, Gus and Dudley, keep her company as she works in her studio.

Glossary

finally (FYE-nuh-lee)—at last

Halloween (hal-oh-EEN)—October 31, believed in the past to be the night when witches and ghosts were active

magician (muh-JISH-uhn)—a person who does tricks

shadow (SHAD-oh)—a dark shape made by something blocking out light

shriek (SHREEK)—a shrill, piercing scream

twirled (TWUR-uhld)—turned or spin around quickly

Discussion Questions

1. How did Katie feel when she couldn't scare anyone while trick-or-treating?

2. Did you think Katie was scary? Why or why not?

3. How do you think Jake felt when he lost his kitty? Have you ever lost something that was special to you? How did you feel?

Writing Prompts

1. Write down three facts you know about Halloween. If you can't think of three, ask a grown-up to help you find some in a book or on the computer.

2. Draw a picture of you in your favorite Halloween costume. Then write a sentence to describe it.

3. Write a list of your five favorite treats to get when you are out trick-or-treating.

Cooking with Katie

Halloween is the perfect time to cook up something spooky. Here is a tasty punch to serve at a creepy costume party. Be sure to ask a grown-up for help, and don't forget to wash your hands!

Witch's Brew

Ingredients:

- 1 quart grape juice
- 1 quart orange juice
- 1 liter ginger ale
- icy hand (see directions on page 32)

Other things you need:

- a punch bowl
- a wooden spoon

What you do:

1. Mix the grape juice and orange juice in the punch bowl. Notice how it turns black . . . YIKES!

2. Just before serving, add the ginger ale.

3. Now for extra creepiness, add the hand.

Icy Hand

What you need:

- a non-powdered, non-latex disposable glove
- water
- a rubber band

What you do:

1. Fill the glove with water.

2. Use the rubber band to seal the glove. Place the glove in the freezer. Freeze overnight.

3. Dip the glove in warm water briefly. Peel off the glove. Now your icy hand is ready for the punch bowl.

Witch's Brew might look pretty gross, but it will taste terrific. It is tricky drink, just for Halloween!

WAIT!

Don't close the book!
There's more!

- Learn more about Katie and her friends
- Find a Katie Woo color sheet, scrapbook, and stationery
- Discover more Katie Woo books

All at . . .

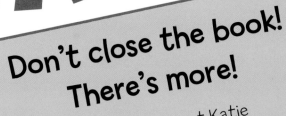

www.capstonekids.com

Still want more?

Find cool websites and more books like this one at www.FACTHOUND.com.

Just type in the **BOOK ID**: 9781404859876 and you're ready to go!